This book belongs to ...

samuel

OXFORD
UNIVERSITY PRESS

Great Clarendon Street,
Oxford, OX2 6DP, United Kingdom

Oxford University Press is a department of the University of Oxford.
It furthers the University's objective of excellence in research, scholarship,
and education by publishing worldwide. Oxford is a registered trade mark
of Oxford University Press in the UK and in certain other countries

British Library Cataloguing in Publication Data
Data available
978-0-19-831027-3

1 3 5 7 9 10 8 6 4 2

Paper used in the production of this book is a natural, recyclable product
made from wood grown in sustainable forests. The manufacturing
process conforms to the environmental regulations of the country of origin.

Printed in China.

Acknowledgements:

Series Editors: Kate Ruttle, Annemarie Young

Shrinking Powder
and Other Stories

The Knight who was Afraid 6

Joe 32

Shrinking Powder 62

Arctic Adventure 92

OXFORD
UNIVERSITY PRESS

Tips for Reading Together

Children learn best when reading is fun.

- Talk about the title and the pictures on the front cover and the title pages of each story.

- Identify the letter pattern *kn* in the title and the letter patterns *kn, n, wr* and *r* in the story, and talk about the sound they make when you read them ('n' as in *not,* and 'r' as in *ran*).

- Look at the words on pages 8 and 9. Say the sound, then read the words (e.g. *kn – knight, n – name, wr – wraps, r – ran*).

- Read the story and find the words with the letter patterns *kn, n, wr* and *r* in them.

- Talk about the story and do the fun activities at the end of the story.

Children enjoy re-reading stories and this helps to build their confidence.

Have fun!

After you have read the story, find the ten rats in the pictures.

The main sounds practised in this book are 'kn' as in *knight* and 'r' as in *ran.*

For more hints and tips on helping your child become a successful and enthusiastic reader look at our website www.oxfordowl.co.uk.

The knight who was Afraid

Written by Roderick Hunt
Illustrated by Nick Schon,
based on the original characters
created by Roderick Hunt and Alex Brychta

OXFORD
UNIVERSITY PRESS

Say the sound and read the words

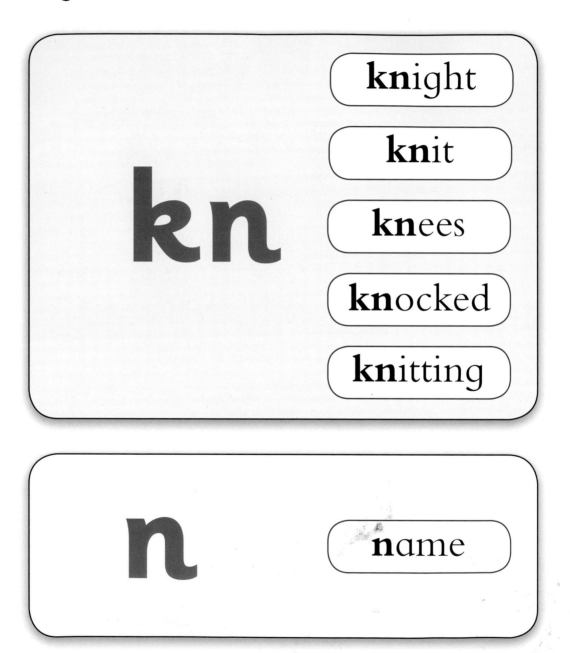

kn

knight

knit

knees

knocked

knitting

n

name

wr

wrote

wraps

r

Ragbag

ran

rats

rot

"I wrote this play," said Wilma.

"I hope you like it."

Dad came onto the stage.

"I am a knight," he said.

My name is Sir Ragbag.

Wilf came onto the stage.

"I am Sir Ragbag's page," he said.

Mum and Biff came on.

"I am Lady Ragbag," said Mum.

"I am the maid," said Biff.

"My name is Kate."

A giant came to the gate.

Jake was afraid.

Kate hid.

"Find a knight to fight me," cried
the giant. "I will lay him out."

Kate ran to Sir Ragbag.

"The giant is on his way," she cried.

Sir Ragbag's face went pale.

His knees knocked.

The giant came.

"I will fight the knight," he cried.

"No, I am a lady," said Sir Ragbag.

"The knight is not in today."

His name is Jane.

"What rot! You are a knight!" cried
the giant. "I will fight you."

Jake had some tame rats.

He let them out.

"I hate rats," cried the giant.

He ran into Lady Ragbag's knitting.

"I was not afraid," said Sir Ragbag.

"That is the end," said Wilma.

"I hope you liked my play."

Talk about the story

Who wrote
the play?

What did
Sir Ragbag do?

Why did the giant
try to run away?

What things
are you afraid of?

27

Word jumble

Make the *kn*, *n*, *r*, and *wr* words from the story.

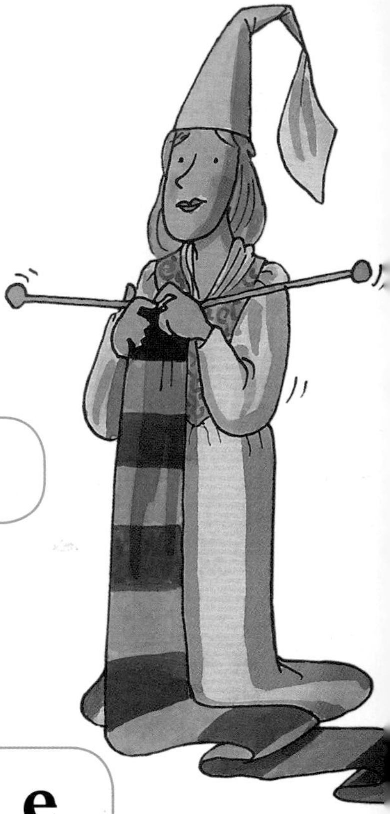

g a b r a g

a r n

s r t a

ing itt kn

m a n e

igh t kn

ck o kn ed

t o e wr

p s wr a

Answers: Ragbag, ran, rats, knitting, name, knight, knocked, wrote, wraps

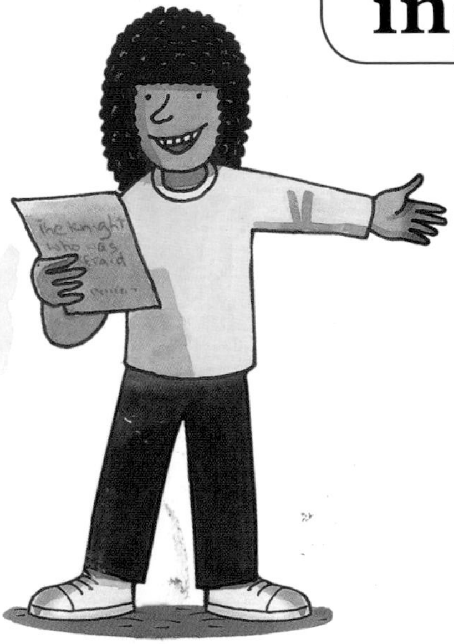

Spot the difference

Find the five differences between the two pictures of the knight.

Word search

Read these words. Can you find them all in the grid?

ragbag

~~knees~~

write

~~rot~~

~~knocked~~

~~knight~~

not

ran

wraps

wrote

nap

v	r	a	g	b	a	g	n	i
a	w	r	i	t	e	t	o	k
j	x	k	n	i	g	h	t	w
q	w	r	a	p	s	n	c	h
r	o	t	r	d	x	n	a	p
o	k	n	e	e	s	h	j	p
q	w	r	o	t	e	o	p	q
t	i	k	n	o	c	k	e	d
r	r	n	o	t	w	r	a	n

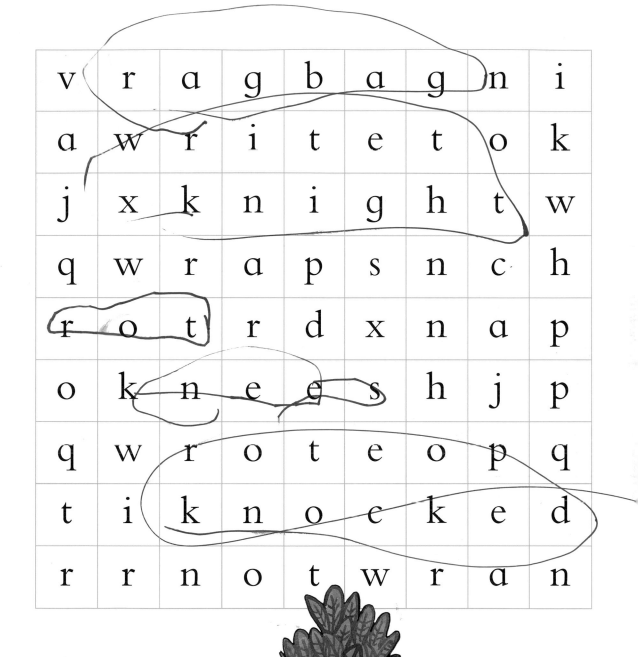

Tips for Reading Together

Children learn best when reading is fun.

- Talk about the title and the pictures on the front cover and the title pages of each story.

- Identify the letter pattern *oe* in the title and the letter patterns *oa*, *o-e*, *ow* and *o*, in the story, and talk about the sound they make when you read them ('oa' as in *coat*).

- Look at the words on pages 34 and 35. Say the sound, then read the words (e.g. *oe – toe*).

- Read the story and find the words with the letter patterns *oe, o-e, ow, oa* and *o* in them.

- Talk about the story and do the fun activities at the end of the story.

Children enjoy re-reading stories and this helps to build their confidence.

 **Have fun!**

After you have read the story, find the five mice in the pictures.

The main sound practised in this book is 'oe' as in *Joe*.

 For more hints and tips on helping your child become a successful and enthusiastic reader look at our website www.oxfordowl.co.uk.

Joe

Written by Roderick Hunt
Illustrated by Nick Schon,
based on the original characters
created by Roderick Hunt and Alex Brychta

OXFORD
UNIVERSITY PRESS

Say the sound and read the words

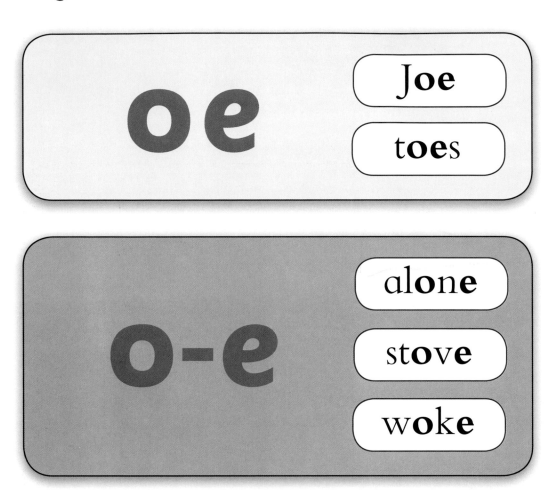

oe

Joe

toes

o-e

alone

stove

woke

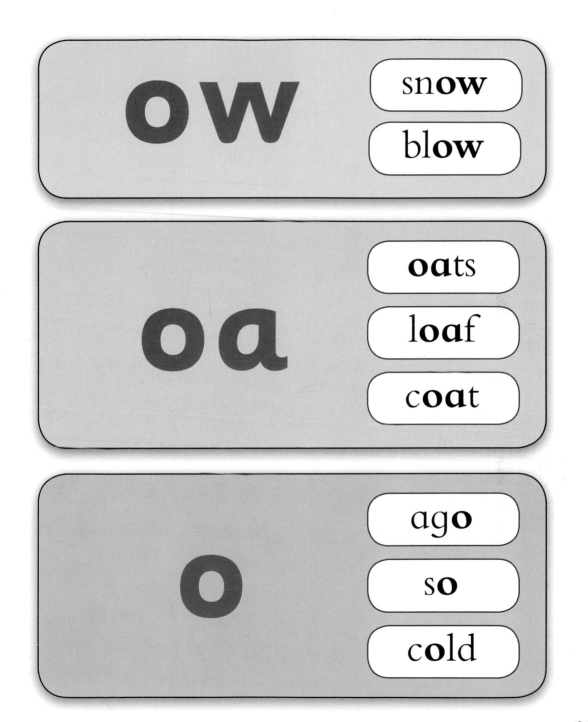

ow

snow

blow

oa

oats

loaf

coat

o

ago

so

cold

"This is Joe," said Chip.

"This is a sad book."

"It was long ago," said Chip.
Joe had no home. He was alone.

He had rips in his coat.

He had holes in his boots and
his toes poked out.

Chip went to sleep.

In his dream he was Joe.

It was snowing.

Joe was cold.

"They keep coal in here," said Joe.
"I'll sleep here by the stove."

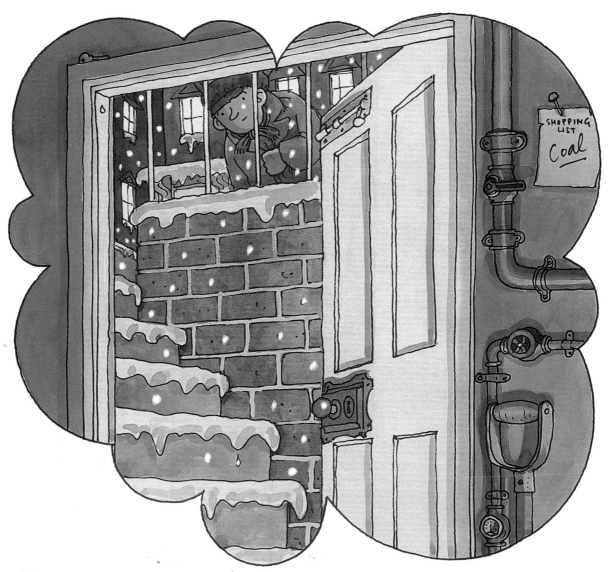

A man came to put coal in the stove.
He woke Joe up.

The man told Joe to go.

Don't come back!

"It's so cold in the snow," said Joe,
"and I need to sleep."

"I am Toby," said a boy.

"This is Rose."

"Eat this bowl of oats," said Rose.

"Put on this coat," said Toby.

"He can eat this loaf," said Rose.

Joe went back in the snow.

Chip woke up. He was cold.

"Tuck me up, Dad," said Chip.
"I don't want to be Joe."

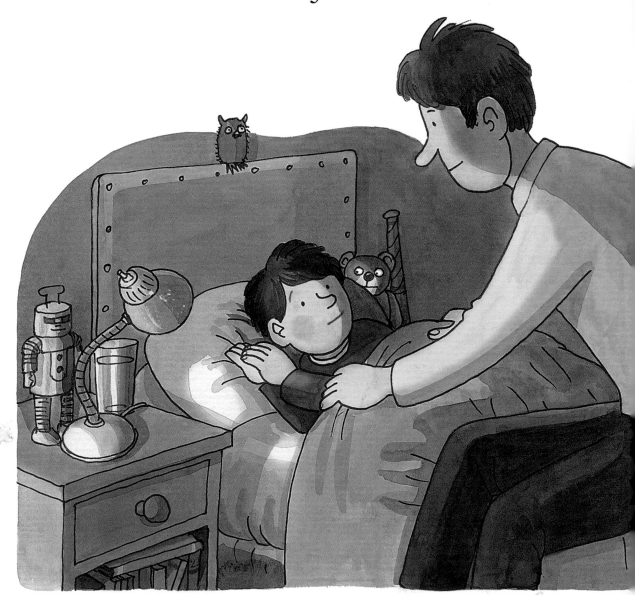

Talk about the story

When did Joe live?

Why did Chip dream that he was Joe?

Why do you think the man told Joe to go?

How were Toby and Rose kind to Joe?

Why didn't Chip want to be Joe?

How have you been kind to someone in trouble?

Word jumble

Make the *oe*, *oa*, *o-e*, *ow* and *o* words from the story.

s oe t

l d o c

ing n ow s

ing o g

Spot the difference

Find the five differences between the two pictures of Joe.

Answer to spot the difference: scarf, hair colour, buttons, pocket, hole in shoe.

Tips for Reading Together

Children learn best when reading is fun.

- Talk about the title and the pictures on the cover and the title pages of each story.

- Discuss what you think the story might be about.

- Read the story together, inviting your child to read as much of it as they can.

- Give lots of praise as your child reads, and help them when necessary.

- Try different ways of helping if they get stuck on a word. For example, get them to say the first sound of the word, or break it into chunks, or read the whole sentence again, trying to guess the word. Focus on the meaning.

- Re-read the story later, encouraging your child to read as much of it as they can.

Children enjoy re-reading stories and this helps to build their confidence.

Have fun!

After you have read the story, find the letters hidden in the pictures that spell out the words SHRINKING POWDER.

This book includes these useful common words:
clothes   everything   laughed   sorry   suddenly

For more hints and tips on helping your child become a successful and enthusiastic reader look at our website www.oxfordowl.co.uk.

Shrinking Powder

Written by Roderick Hunt
Illustrated by Alex Brychta

OXFORD
UNIVERSITY PRESS

Dad did the washing, but he put the
clothes on a hot wash.

"Oh no!" said Dad. "The clothes
have shrunk."

"Look at my top," said Kipper.

"Look at my jeans," said Biff.

"Sorry," said Dad. "I forgot to set the washing machine. It was too hot."

Chip made a little boy with the clothes that had shrunk.

"That's a good joke," laughed Biff.

Suddenly, the magic key began to glow. It took the children into an adventure.

The key took them to a shop.
It sold magic tricks and strange things.

"Wow!" said Chip. "It's a joke shop.
But there's nobody here. I think the
shop is shut."

Suddenly, there was a loud POP
and a puff of purple smoke.
"What's that?" asked Chip.

72

A boy was standing in the shop.

"I'm sorry about all the smoke,"
he said.

"I'm Jake," said the boy. "I'm
learning to be a wizard.
Watch this."

"Hooray! It works," said Jake, "but learning to be a wizard is not easy."

Jake took a tin out of his pocket.

"I want to try this," he said.

"It's shrinking powder," said Jake.

"I want to see if it works."

He shook some over Kipper.

Kipper began to shrink. "Help!"
he said. "Everything looks big."

"Hooray!" said Jake. "It works!"

"Oh no!" said Biff and Chip.

"Kipper has shrunk."

"It's not funny," said Kipper.

Jake tapped Kipper with a wand.

"Now I'll make him big," he said.

Suddenly, Kipper had huge ears.
"Whoops!" said Jake. "That's not
quite right ... let me try again."

Jake waved the wand. Suddenly,
Kipper had long, green hair.
"This is *not* funny," said Kipper.

Jake waved the wand again.

"I *am* sorry," said Jake. "I can't make him big."

Chip was cross. He took Jake's
wand. "Let *me* try," he said.
Just then, the key glowed.

The key took them back. Kipper's
big ears and green hair had gone,
but he was still small.

"Dad is coming," said Chip.

"We can't let him see Kipper."

"Let's put a box on him," said Biff.

Suddenly, Kipper was big again.

"What are you up to?" asked Dad.

"Shrinking Kipper," said Biff.

"That's a good joke!" laughed
Dad.

Talk about the story

How did Jake make Kipper shrink?

What went wrong?

How did Kipper feel when he had shrunk?

Which magic tricks have you seen?

Jake's mistakes - rhyming pairs

Jake has put the wrong labels on the pictures.
Can you find the right ones?

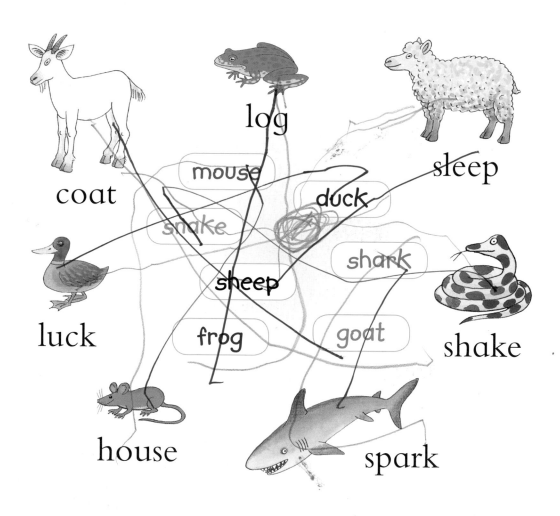

log

coat

mouse

duck

sleep

snake

shark

sheep

luck

frog

goat

shake

house

spark

Answers: coat – goat, log – frog, sleep – sheep, shake – snake,
spark – shark, house – mouse, luck – duck.

Tips for Reading Together

Children learn best when reading is fun.

- Talk about the title and the pictures on the cover and the title pages of each story.

- Discuss what you think the story might be about.

- Read the story together, inviting your child to read as much of it as they can.

- Give lots of praise as your child reads, and help them when necessary.

- Try different ways of helping if they get stuck on a word. For example, get them to say the first sound of the word, or break it into chunks, or read the whole sentence again. Focus on the meaning.

- Re-read the story later, encouraging your child to read as much of it as they can.

Children enjoy re-reading stories **Have fun!** and this helps to build their confidence.

After you have read the story, find the letters in the pictures that spell out the words POLAR BEAR.

This book includes these useful common words:
clothes   everywhere   glad   soon   suddenly

For more hints and tips on helping your child become a successful and enthusiastic reader look at our website www.oxfordowl.co.uk.

Arctic Adventure

Written by Roderick Hunt
Illustrated by Alex Brychta

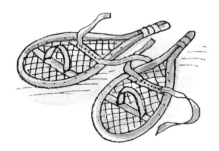

OXFORD
UNIVERSITY PRESS

THE POLAR BEAR

Wilf was staying with Chip. It was
very hot.

"It's too hot to sleep," said Chip.

"I wish we were in the Arctic,"
said Wilf. "It's cold there."

Suddenly, the magic key began to
glow. It took them into an adventure.

The key took Chip and Wilf to the
Arctic. There was snow everywhere.

The snow felt cold. "Brrrr!" said
Chip. "Now, I'm freezing."

Wilf saw a girl. "Help!" he called.

"We are freezing in this snow."

The girl came over. "You need some
warm clothes," she said.

"My name is Oona," said the girl.
"Put these clothes on."

"Now you can help me catch
some fish," said Oona.

"You can't catch fish in the snow,"
said Chip.

"I can," said Oona.

There was ice under the snow.
Under the ice was the sea. Oona
made a hole and they started to fish.

Soon, they had five fish.

Suddenly, Chip saw a polar bear.

"Run!" he gasped. "It's going to
eat us!"

106

Chip and Wilf ran.

"It's hard to run in the snow,"
panted Wilf.

"Stop!" called Oona. "The bear just wants some fish."

"She's only a cub, and she's lost,"
said Oona. "I've been helping my
dad to find her."

The cub ate the fish and soon
fell asleep.

"I'll call Dad now," said Oona.

Oona's dad came. "Well done,
Oona," he said. "Now we can get the
cub back to her mother."

They put the cub on a sled and
set off across the snow.

"The cub needs her mother,"
said Oona. "She hasn't learned
to hunt yet."

They saw a big polar bear on the ice.
"Is that her mother?" asked Wilf.

The mother bear gave a roar.
Then she dived into the sea and
swam to her cub.

"I'm glad we helped the cub find her mother," said Oona.

"I'm glad I'm not a polar bear!"
said Chip.

Just then, the key began to glow.

"That was a cold adventure,"
said Wilf.

"But it's still hot!" said Chip.

Talk about the story

How did Oona catch the fish?

Why did the bear cub need her mother?

Why do you think people want to help polar bears?

If you were very hot, how would you cool down? If you were very cold, how would you keep warm?

A maze

Help the mother polar bear find her way to her cub.

Read with Biff, Chip and Kipper
The UK's best-selling home reading series

Phonics **First Stories**

	Phonics	First Stories
Level 1 Getting ready to read	Kipper's Alphabet I Spy · Chip's Letter Sounds · Biff's Wonder Words · Biff's Fun Phonics · Kipper's Rhymes · Floppy's Fun Phonics	Get On · Floppy Did This! · Up You Go · The Pancake · A Good Trick · Six in a Bed
Level 2 Starting to read	I am Kipper · Cat in a Bag · The Red Hen · Win a Nut · A Yak at the Picnic · The Fizz-Buzz	Funny Fish · Silly Races! · The Snowman · Mum's New Hat · Picnic Time · Dad's Birthday
Level 3 Becoming a reader	Such a Fuss · Shops · The Sing Song · The Backpack	Poor Old Rabbit · I Can Trick a Tiger · Super Dad · Floppy and the Bone
Level 4 Developing as a reader	Wet Feet · The Moon Jet · The Red Coat · Quick! Quick!	Missing! · Raft Race · Dragon Danger · The Spaceship
Level 5 Building confidence in reading	Egg Fried Rice · Craig Saves the Day · Seasick · Dolphin Rescue	Hungry Floppy · Husky Adventure · Trapped! · Looking after Gran
Level 6 Reading with confidence	Gran's New Blue Shoes · Ice City · Save Pudding Wood · Uncle Max	Hairy-Scary Monster · Mountain Rescue · The Lost Voice · Secret of the Sands

Phonics stories help children practise their sounds and letters, as they learn to do in school.

First Stories have been specially written to provide practice in reading everyday language.

Read with Biff, Chip and Kipper Collections:

Up You Go and Other Stories · Kipper's Rhymes and other Stories · Six in a Bed and other Stories · Funny Fish and Other Stories · Picnic Time and other Stories · The Fizz-Buzz and Other Stories · Floppy and the Bone and Other Stories

I Can Trick a Tiger and Other Stories · The Moon Jet and Other Stories · Dragon Danger and Other Stories · Husky Adventure and Other Stories · Looking After Gran and Other Stories · Hairy-Scary Monster and Other Stories · Secret of the Sands and Other Stories

2 Phonics and 2 First Stories in every collection

Phonics support

Flashcards are a really fun way to practise phonics and build reading skills. **Age 3+**

My Phonics Kit is designed to support you and your child as you practise phonics together at home. It includes stickers, workbooks, interactive eBooks, support for parents and more! **Age 5+**

Read Write Inc. Phonics: A range of fun rhyming stories to support decoding skills. **Age 4+**

Songbirds Phonics: Lively and engaging phonics stories from former Children's Laureate, Julia Donaldson. **Age 4+**

Helping your child's learning with free eBooks, essential tips and fun activities
www.oxfordowl.co.uk